DEDICATED TO

Lozza
Prudence
Stephen
Suzanne
Cherie

cajvcbb.studio@gmail.com
Illustrations by CAJ WHITING
Cover design by CAJ WHITING
ISBN: 9798345271742
Published by: Independently Published

THIS BOOK
BELONGS TO

· ·

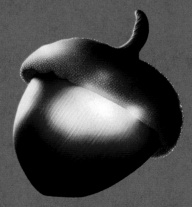

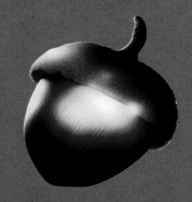

"It's not that I'm so smart; it's just that I stay with problems longer." – Albert Einstein

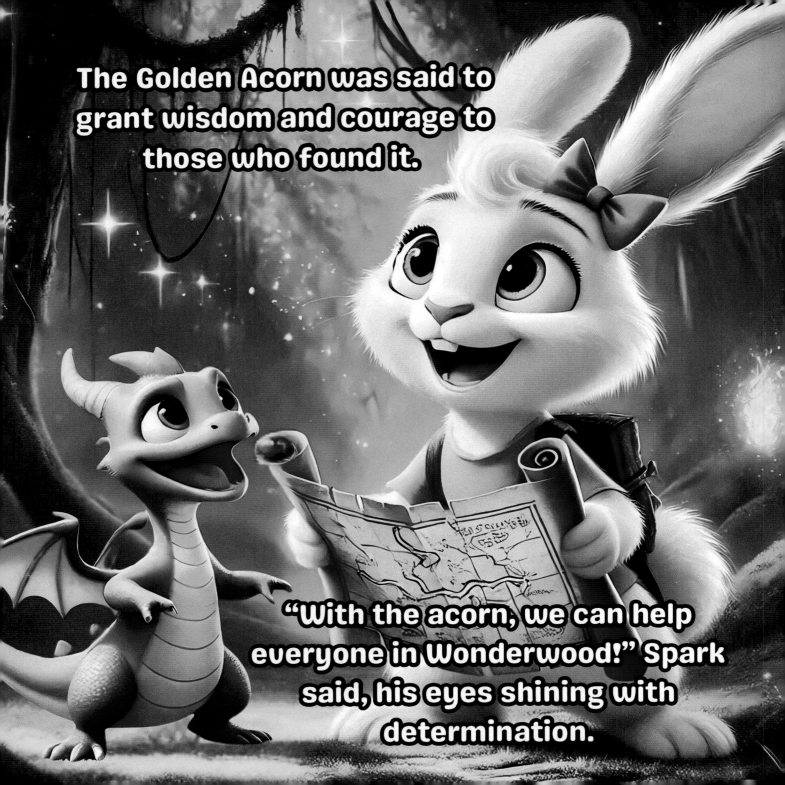

They packed their bags with snacks and supplies, ready for the journey. "It won't be easy." Belle warned.

"But we won't give up!" Spark nodded, knowing perseverance was the key to finding the acorn.

As they ventured deeper into the forest, the path became tricky. First, they faced a stream with slippery rocks.

Belle tried to cross but slipped. "I can't do it!" she said, feeling frustrated.

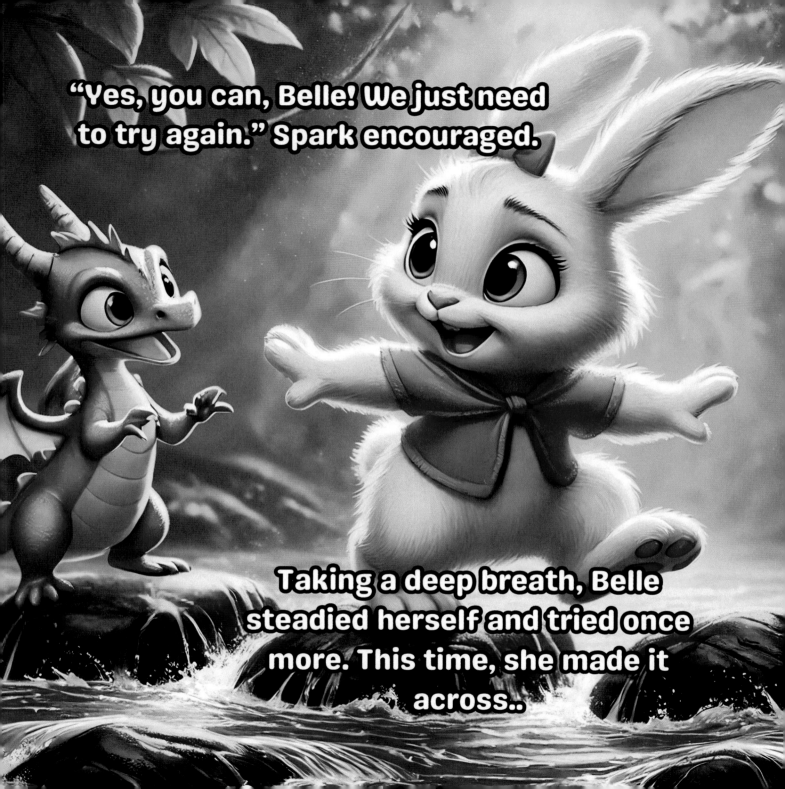

Next, they came upon a steep hill covered in loose gravel. "This is impossible!" Spark exclaimed, slipping back after each step.

But Belle, still determined, said, "We have to keep trying. We can't give up now."

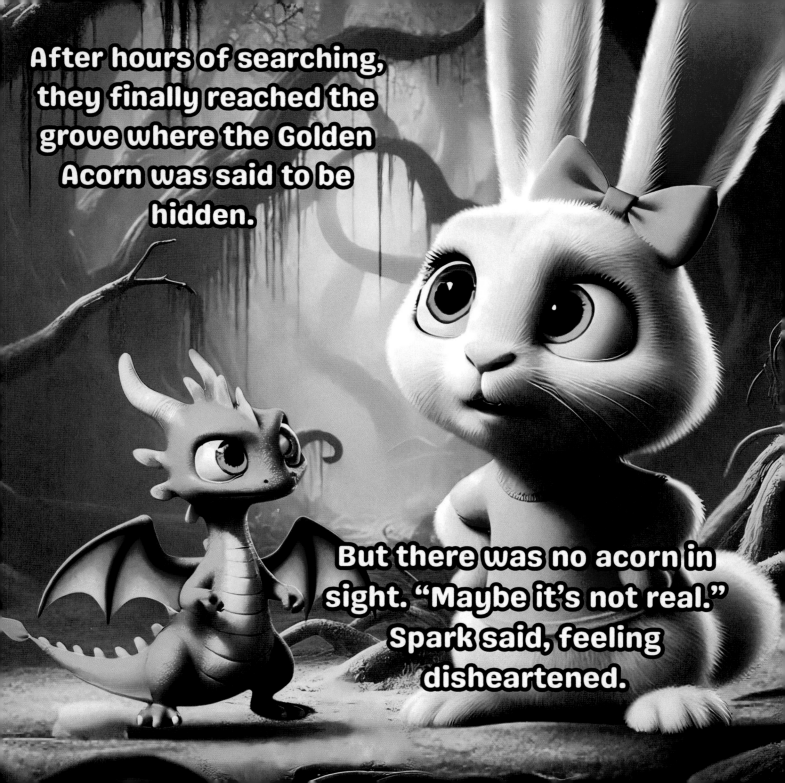

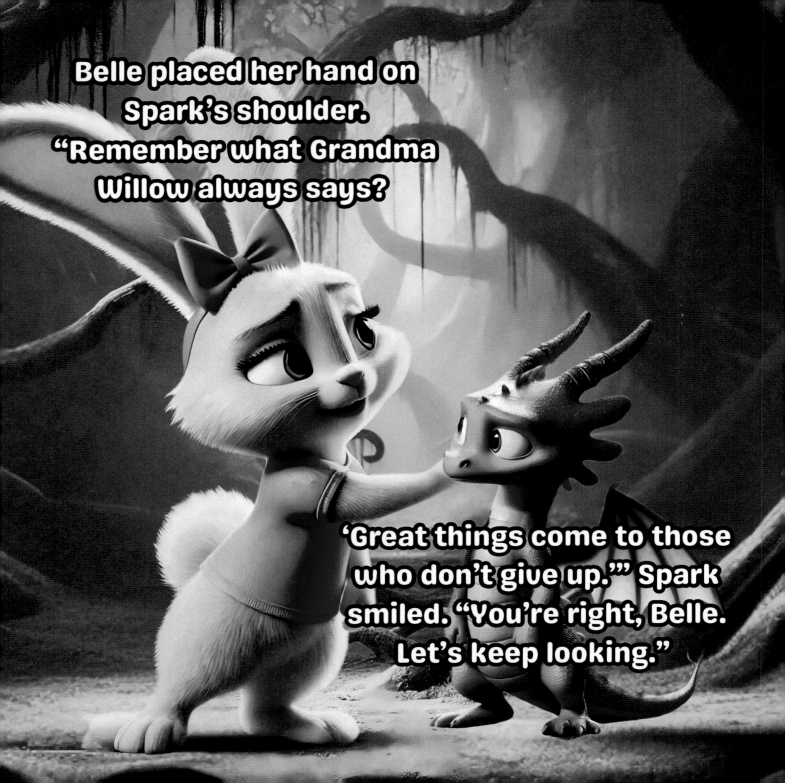

Just when they were about to lose hope, Spark noticed a glimmer under some leaves. "Belle! Look!" he cried.

Under the leaves, they found the Golden Acorn, shining brightly.

As they walked back home, Belle and Spark felt proud. They learned that with perseverance, anything was possible.

Belle and Spark returned to Wonderwood as heroes, ready to face any challenge together.

As they settled in for the night, they knew perseverance was the most powerful tool they had.

Lets Talk
Parent-Child Discussion

Why was it important for Belle and Spark to keep trying even when things got tough?

This question encourages children to think about the value of persistence.
It helps them understand that challenges are a natural part of any journey and that perseverance can lead to success.

Can you think of a time when you didn't give up, and it paid off?

This question helps children make personal connections to the story.
By reflecting on their own experiences, they recognize the positive outcomes of their perseverance.

How can you use perseverance to achieve your goals?

This question encourages children to apply the lesson to future situations. It teaches them to set goals and understand that perseverance is key to reaching those goals.

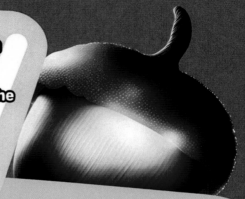

Parent-Child Discussion Notes

USE THIS PAGE TO RECORD AND COMPARE THE ANSWERS GIVEN ON DIFFERENT OCCASIONS TO SEE HOW YOUR CHILD IS DEVELOPING (RECOMMENDED 3- 6 MONTH INTERVALS)

Additional Notes

ACTIVITY TIME

I Can't...Yet! Challenge:

Have children draw something they think they can't do yet. Underneath the drawing, write 'I can't...yet' to reinforce the power of perseverance. This activity encourages children to visualize their challenges and use a growth mindset to believe in future improvement.

Acorn Hunt

Hide acorns (or small objects) around your home or yard and have a "perseverance hunt" where children must search until they find them all. This activity helps children practice perseverance in a fun, engaging way. It reinforces the idea that even when something seems challenging, continued effort can lead to success.

Perseverance Storytime

Have children share stories about a time they didn't give up, and celebrate their perseverance just like Belle and Spark did. This activity encourages children to reflect on their own experiences, promoting self-awareness. Sharing their stories helps build confidence and reinforces the value of perseverance.

I Can't .....YET.

I can't ....YET!
But soon I will.

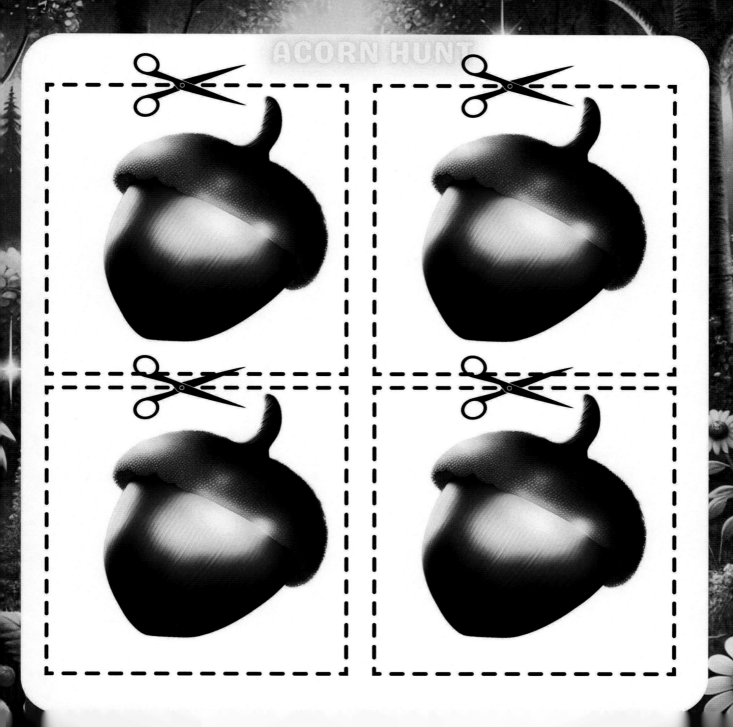

Goals

Encourage the child to set goals in order to achieve something they can't do.....YET

_____

Goal 1. _____

_____

_____

Goal 2. _____

_____

Goal 3. _____

_____

_____

I Can't...

YET!

I Can't...

YET!

I Can't...

YET!

5 Ways to Incorporate SEL with "Belle & Spark - The Power of Perseverance"

Here are five ways parents can incorporate Social-Emotional Learning (SEL) while reading Belle and Spark: The Power of Perseverance with their children:

1. Pause for Reflection
Pause at key moments to ask questions like, "How do you think Belle feels?" or "What would you do if you were Spark?" This helps children develop empathy by analyzing the characters' feelings.

2. Connect to Real Life
Encourage your child to share a time they faced a tough situation. Ask, "Can you think of a time when you kept going even though it was hard?" Relating challenges to real life helps children understand perseverance.

3. Practice Positive Self-Talk
When Belle and Spark face obstacles, discuss how they might use positive self-talk. Ask, "What could Belle say to stay determined?" Encourage phrases like, "I can do this!" Practicing positive self-talk strengthens resilience.

4. Set a Goal Together
After reading, set a small, achievable goal your child can work toward. Track their progress, similar to how Belle and Spark overcame challenges. This teaches perseverance through setting and achieving goals.

5. Problem-Solving Role Play
Re-enact scenes where Belle and Spark face challenges, letting your child explore different solutions. Ask, "What would you try if you were Spark?" Role-playing encourages problem-solving in a safe space.

These activities make SEL lessons interactive and meaningful, helping children understand perseverance as they engage with the story.

Notes

THANK YOU FOR JOINING BELLE & SPARK ON THEIR ADVENTURE!

We hope you enjoyed *Belle & Spark: The Power of Perseverance* and learned about the importance of perseverance just like Belle and Spark did. Remember, perseverance helps us overcome challenges—like learning to ride a bike or finishing a difficult puzzle—and achieve our goals.

TIPS FOR PARENTS AND CAREGIVERS

Talk to your children about perseverance using simple, relatable examples from daily life, such as learning to tie their shoes or complete a challenging homework assignment. Encourage them to keep trying, whether it's tying shoelaces, solving a puzzle, or practicing a skill. These small victories build resilience and confidence, helping them grow stronger with each effort.

STAY TUNED FOR MORE ADVENTURES!

Belle and Spark will be back with more exciting adventures—maybe they'll tackle a new challenge in Wonderwood! Keep exploring, keep learning, and always believe in yourself.

WE VALUE YOUR FEEDBACK!

If you enjoyed this book, please consider leaving a review on Amazon. Your feedback helps us reach more readers and continue to share Belle and Spark's wonderful adventures.

MORE ADVENTURES AWAIT!

Discover the other books in the *Belle & Spark* series for more fun, learning, and valuable life lessons. Each story brings a new journey filled with magic and important messages.

JOIN OUR COMMUNITY!

We would love for you to join our growing community! Follow us on Facebook for updates, activities, exclusive sneak peeks, and special offers: [Just search for Belle & Spark on Facebook you'll recognize us]

#BelleAndSpark #PerseverancePaysOff #ChildrensBooks #SEL